that
pesky
rat

lauren child

ORCHARD BOOKS

Thank you
Randala
and Albena

Look out for Lauren Child's
Clarice Bean books
and the award-winning
I will not ever
NEVER
eat a tomato

Max

and for anyone who
has ever wished they
were somebody's pet

Sam

Lucy

Zaida

and for fabulous
Frances and her
pets Lucy, Sam,
Ata and Cui

Louie

This book is for
the gorgeous Max
and her little
dog Louie

Flame

Sita

Ata & Cui

Twinkle

with love to Jo and Thomas,
long-suffering owners of Twinkle,
the Bette Davis of cats

Cheeky

Donut

ORCHARD BOOKS
338 Euston Road, London NW1 3BH
Orchard Books Australia
Hachette Children's Books
Level 17/207 Kent Street,
Sydney, NSW 2000
First published in 2002
by Orchard Books
First paperback publication in 2003
ISBN-10: 1 84121 830 8 (HB)
ISBN-13: 978 1 84121 830 4 (HB)
ISBN-10: 1 84121 276 8 (PB)
ISBN-13: 978 1 84121 276 0 (PB)
Copyright © Lauren Child 2002

The right of Lauren Child to be identified as the author
and illustrator of this work has been asserted by her in
accordance with the Copyright, Designs and Patents Act,
1988. A CIP catalogue record for this book is available
from the British Library
10 9 8
Printed in Singapore
Orchard Books is a division of Hachette Children's Books

This is me.
I'm the one with the **pointy**
nose and b e a d y eyes.
The cutesy one
in the middle.

I live in
dustbin
number **3**,
Grubby
Alley.

Every now and again I come back to find
someone has emptied all my belongings
into a **big** van and driven off with them.
It's very **upsetting.**

I'm a brown rat, a street rat.
But people call me that pesky rat.
I don't know why.
They say I smell,
but that's not my fault, it's the dirt.

Sometimes when I am tucked into
my crisp packet,
I look up at all the cosy windows
and wonder what it would be like
to live with creature comforts.
To belong to somebody.
To be an actual pet.

Most of all I would like

to have a **name**, instead of just that *pesky rat*.

My friend Pierre, who is a **chinchilla**, is looked after by a rich lady called Madame Fifi.

He has a very **glamorous** life.

He lives in the lap of luxury.

I hate having baths.

I think I'm **allergic** to soap.

Then there's this
Siamese cat
called Oscar.
He lives with
Mr Washington,
a busy businessman.

Mr Washington
is always at work
so he doesn't have
time to wash fur
or be strict.

Oscar says,
"Doing whatever you want can get tiring after a while. I sometimes get a bit **bored** watching the **same old shows** on TV.

even

I

have

to

get my

own

supper."

Swinging on the trapeze one minute, tip-toeing on the high wire the next.

Maybe it's all a bit nerve wracking for me.

I think I'd quite like one of those owners
who do lots of **sitting about**
like **Miss StClair.**

Her **Scottie** dog, Andrew, is **always** sitting by the

fire, having supper on a tray and they spend the evenings doing Puzzles together.

Andrew says,

"On the whole I feel **very well** looked after.

And Miss StClair is good company.

But it's rather **embarrassing** when we go out shopping."

Miss StClair makes **Andrew** wear a little **hat** and coat.

So in the morning
I go to the pet shop
and ask Mrs Trill

if she has

an owner

who might **want** me.

She says,

"There isn't much call for brown rats, and I'm afraid you aren't very popular with the public."

I say,

"I don't see why not. I'm very good company, always popping up when you least expect me to, and I am happy to eat anything, even if it's been slightly nibbled."

Mrs Trill says,

"Well, you could always make a notice and put it in the window. You never know."

So I write:

Me →

Brown cat looking for kindly owner
with an interest in cheese
Hobbies include nibbling and chewing
would like a collar with my name on
would like a name
would prefer no baths
will wear a jumper if pushed
Yours keenly
        Brown cat (that pesky cat)

P.S sorry about bad paw writing

not
a very good picture

Then I wait and I wait

and   I   wait.   Until . . .

. . . on Tuesday old **Mr Fortesque** is passing
and he **stops** to look at my **notice.**

He has to really **squint** because he
has such **bad** eyesight.

Then he looks at me and says,

"My,
haven't you
got a pointy nose
and, goodness me,
what a long tail, and such
unusual beady eyes . . .

I'll take him."

I can't
believe my **luck,**
nor can Mrs Trill.

Mrs Trill says,
"Are you sure?"

And Mr Fortesque says,
"Oh yes, I've been looking for a brown cat
as nice as this one for ages."

Mrs Trill looks at me and I look at Mrs Trill,
and we both look at my notice,

but neither of us
says a word.

I just **love** being a **pet.**
And . . . I am trying to be **really** helpful.

I pick out the best **cheeses**
by using my excellent sniffing nose.

I clean the kitchen
by n i b b l i n g
up the
c r u m b s.

I help Mr Fortesque

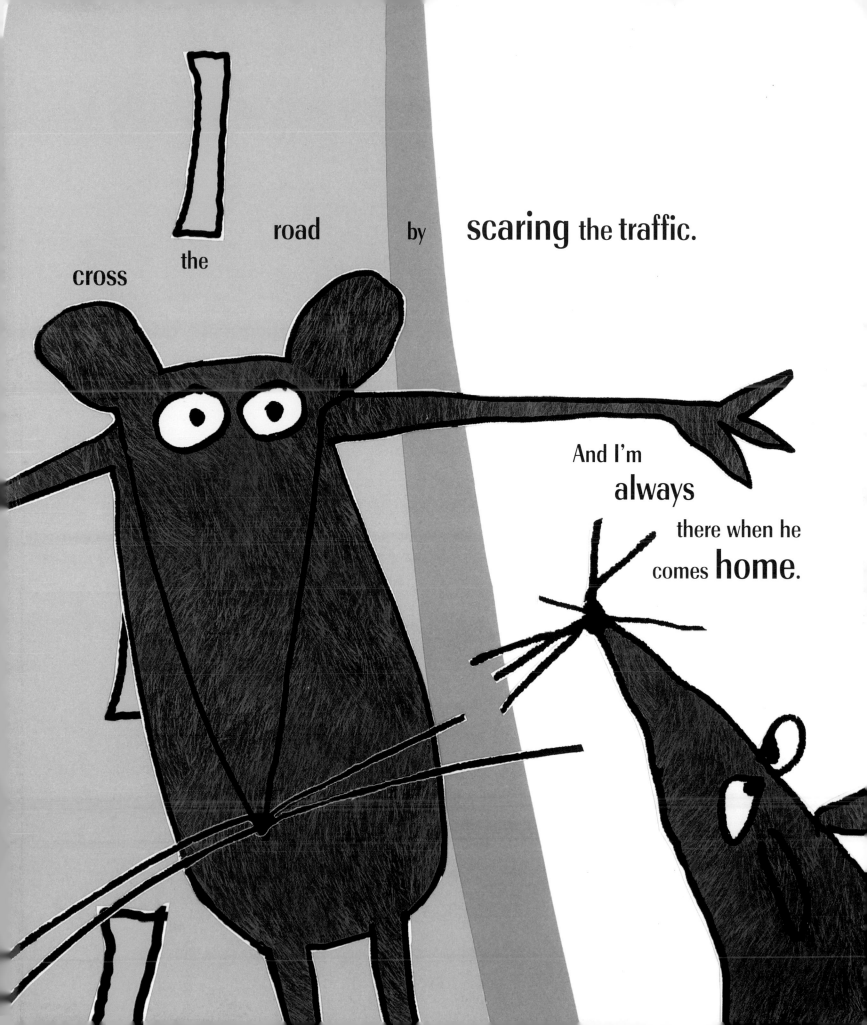

So here I am.

Finally a pet with a name.

So what if I have to wear a little jumper?

Mr Fortesque says, "Well, Tiddles, who's a pretty kittycat?"

And I squeak, "I am!"